There Was an Old Woman Who Lived in a Shoe

The Child's World®

Distributed by The Child's World®
1980 Lookout Drive • Mankato, MN 56003-1705
800-599-READ • www.childsworld.com

Acknowledgments
The Child's World®: Mary Berendes, Publishing Director
The Design Lab: Kathleen Petelinsek, Design

Library of Congress Cataloging-in-Publication Data
Marten, Luanne Voltmer.
 There was an old woman who lived in a shoe /
illustrated by Luanne Marten.
     p. cm.
 ISBN 978-1-60954-284-9 (library bound: alk. paper)
 1. Nursery rhymes. 2. Children's poetry. [1. Nursery rhymes.] I. Title.
 PZ8.3.M3987Th 2011
 398.8—dc22
 [E]   2010032419

Printed in the United States of America in Mankato, Minnesota.
December 2010
PA02073

ILLUSTRATED BY LUANNE MARTEN

There was
an old woman
who lived
in a shoe.

5

She had so many children,
she didn't know what to do.

So she gave them some broth,

with plenty of bread.

She kissed them all sweetly
and put them to bed.

13

ABOUT MOTHER GOOSE

We all remember the Mother Goose nursery rhymes we learned as children. But who was Mother Goose, anyway? Did she even exist? The answer is . . . we don't know! Many different tales surround this famous name.

Some people think she might be based on Goose-footed Bertha, a kindly old woman in French legend who told stories to children. The inspiration for this legend might have been Queen Bertha of France, who died in 783 and whose son Charlemagne ruled much of Europe. Queen Bertha was called Big-footed Bertha or Queen Goosefoot because one foot was larger than the other.

The name "Mother Goose" first appeared in Charles Perrault's *Les Contes de ma Mère l'Oye* ("Tales of My Mother Goose"), published in France in 1697. This was a collection of fairy tales including "Cinderella" and "Sleeping Beauty"—but these were stories, not poems. The first published Mother Goose nursery rhymes appeared in England in 1781, as *Mother Goose's Melody; or Sonnets for the Cradle.* But some of the verses themselves are hundreds of years old, passed along by word of mouth.

Although we don't really know the origins of Mother Goose or her nursery rhymes, we *do* know that these timeless verses are beloved by children everywhere!

ABOUT THE ILLUSTRATOR

Luanne Marten loves to draw! She enjoys creating illustrations on the computer, paper, canvas, and even with her sewing machine. When she is not making art, Luanne loves to read and play the piano. She lives in Kansas City with her husband and is the mother of four grown sons.